ERIC AND THE STRIPED HORROR

by
Barbara
Mitchelhill

illustrated by
Bridget
MacKeith

RED FOX

To Anne Williams, Pam Pollitt
and Gordon Dickens and the splendid team
of the Shropshire Library Services

Chapter 1

Eric Braithwaite suddenly woke up and saw The Bodge leaning over him.

'I know you're half asleep,' The Bodge growled, 'so I'll repeat it especially for you.'

'Me, Sir? I wasn't asleep – honest! I was thinking . . . about the final . . . and our strategies.'

The Bodge was not impressed – not even by the word 'strategies'. 'I shouldn't get too excited about football if I were you.'

'But we're going to win, Sir. It'll be the first time ever we've beaten that lot at Woodthorne.'

Whispered cheers went up round the room and grinning faces turned in Eric's direction.

'We'll get the County Cup and we'll be dead famous,' he babbled. 'On the telly and everything. We'll give interviews, Sir, and they'll all want our autographs. I've always wanted to be a famous footballer . . .'

'STOP!' yelled The Bodge. 'You won't be winning anything, my lad, unless you do well in tomorrow's test.' And he stormed to the front of the class.

'Test?' echoed Eric. 'What test?' And he turned to his mate, Wesley, expecting an answer.

The Bodge's face was slowly changing to a deep shade of purple as it always did when he was in a temper. 'The rest of the class ALREADY KNOW ABOUT THE TEST!' he shouted. 'So would you if you hadn't been asleep. NOW LISTEN! Tomorrow morning you'll be having a test covering all this term's work.'

Eric wondered why he was making such a big deal about it. It was just another test, wasn't it? Unless there was a catch somewhere.

There was.

'Anyone getting less than 40 out of 100,' The Bodge continued, 'will have extra tuition from the Head.'

Eric groaned. He would probably be one of them. Spending hours with Mrs Cracker – known as The Big Cheese – would be grim. He'd faint with the pong of her perfume. She had two – 'Essence of Old Socks' and 'Souvenir de Gorgonzola'.

Eric put his hand up. 'Sir! What if we're sick and have to miss the test?'

The Bodge ignored him and continued. 'The extra tuition will take place during games lessons,' he said, 'and for an hour after school – for three weeks.'

Eric leapt to his feet and shot his arm in the air. 'That doesn't include matches does it, Sir?'

'It includes PE, games and all matches – football, netball . . . everything,' The Bodge insisted. 'You will have to miss them for those three weeks. IS THAT CLEAR, ERIC?'

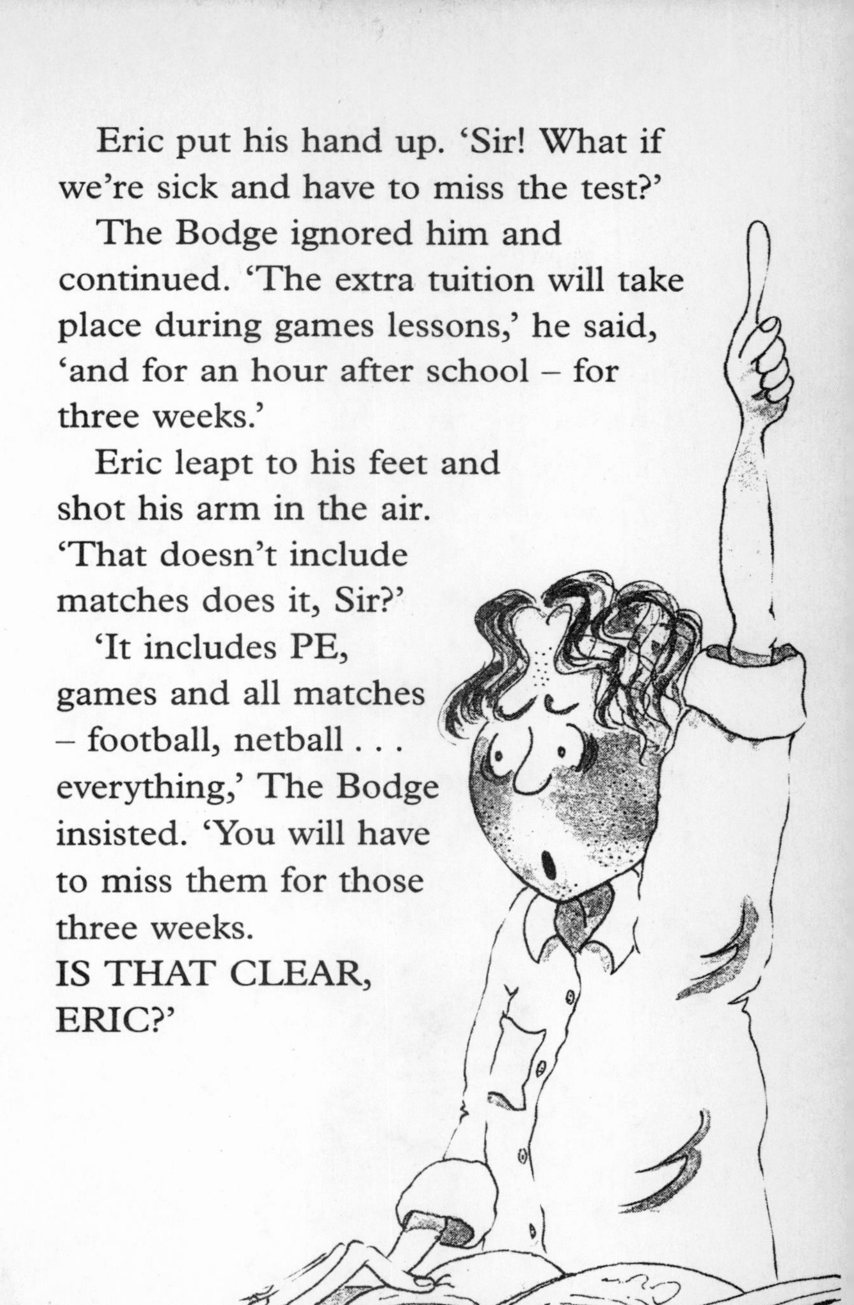

It was very clear – and Eric sat down with a thump. A stunned silence filled the room, followed by a distinct ripple of grizzling groans. The Junior Football Final was less than two weeks away and Eric was the captain and a striker. If he had to stay behind, they had no chance of winning.

So what was he going to do about it?

Chapter 2

On the way home, Eric talked with Wesley about the test.

'I know I won't get 40,' he groaned. 'I haven't had time to do any studying this term, have I? Been too busy training and planning tactics to do the homework. Always copied yours, didn't I?'

Wesley nodded and kicked the toe of his boot against the wall. 'We'll never win without you, Ez. We don't stand a chance. That stuck-up lot from Woodthorne'll get the cup. They ALWAYS win. This was the first time we've had a hope.'

Eric glowered at the pavement. 'Real sneaky of The Bodge to go testing us like that,' he moaned. 'I'm sick as a parrot!' and then, stuffing his hands deep into his pockets, he left Wesley and turned down Corporation Street.

When he got home, Mum was cooking bacon. (She was brilliant with a frying pan – but not much else, really.)

'Go and read your school books, duck,' she said when he told her about the test. 'An hour or two studying could work wonders. Give the telly a miss for once. You watch too much anyway.'

Eric leaned against the back door feeling more fed up than ever. No telly? He'd die – especially when the United match was on LIVE!

Mum opened a tin of tomatoes and put them in with the bacon. 'By the way,' she said, 'there's a parcel for you on the hall table.'

Eric raced to the door. 'It'll be my birthday present from Auntie Rose. I've been waiting for it. She's always late.'

'I'm surprised they ever get here at all, the places she gets to,' Mum called out from the kitchen. 'How far's it come this time?'

'South America,' Eric yelled from the hall.

It was wrapped in brown paper and addressed in Rose's unmistakable bold black writing. Five stamps were stuck in the corner, post-marked *Cali – Rep. of Colombia*.

All of a rush, he tore it open. Was it a football strip? Was it a pair of shorts? Was it a baseball cap? Something brown and yellow and orange appeared and, as he pulled it out of the paper, a stink of goats . . .

or camel dung . . . or rotting cabbage came with it. He held his nose in one hand and the striped thing in the other. It was a peculiar, woolly jumper.

'That's weird,' Eric said to himself and tossed it aside on the hall table. As he did, a piece of blue paper fell at his feet. It was a letter from Auntie Rose which he unfolded and read:

Dear Freckle Face,

Hope you had a fantastic birthday. How's it feel to be an old man?

South America is brilliant. Wherever I go, I have adventures and meet the most amazing people. If I survive, I'll tell you all about it when I get home – which should be in two months' time. I hope you like your present. It was given to me by a tribe of people living in the foothills of the Andes (very high, the Andes!). They are descendants of the Chibcha Indians and dye all their own wool from natural dyes. Do you like the colours? I think they're terrific!

But wait till you hear this!

I was told that the wool comes from the sheep on a mystical part of the Andes and that the jumper has special powers. Isn't that spooky? That's what they told me – unless I got the translation wrong. The woman who made it said it

Dear Freckle
Hope you
tastic bi
it fee

would improve the wearer's brain power (some hopes!). But its powers would only last as long as it wasn't washed. I didn't think you'd mind about that! I know you're not keen on washing!

Enjoy wearing it.

Have you been signed up to play for United yet? Keep practising!

Love and a kiss,
Auntie Rose.

Eric looked once more at the jumper. 'The Striped Horror of South America!' he said. 'I wouldn't dare wear it! I'd look a real twit!' Then he raced upstairs, stuffed it under his bed and forgot about it.

Chapter 3

Just to please his mum, Eric sacrificed an evening in front of the telly and went up to his room to study. It was not something he did often and so it was not surprising that he felt the strain after twenty minutes.

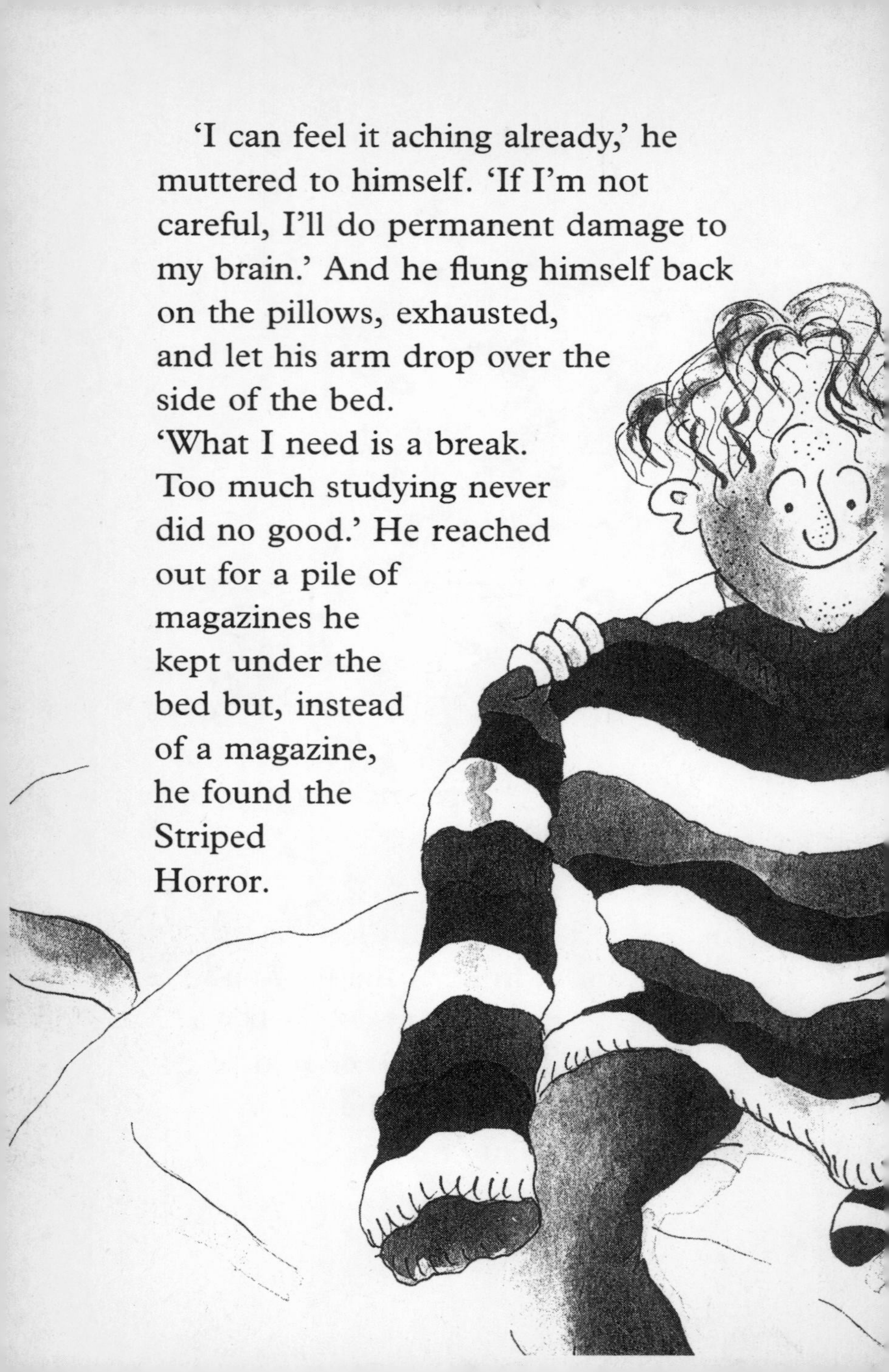

'I can feel it aching already,' he muttered to himself. 'If I'm not careful, I'll do permanent damage to my brain.' And he flung himself back on the pillows, exhausted, and let his arm drop over the side of the bed. 'What I need is a break. Too much studying never did no good.' He reached out for a pile of magazines he kept under the bed but, instead of a magazine, he found the Striped Horror.

Annoyed, he pushed it to one side, but at the same time, an idea came to him that was so brilliant that he sat bolt upright on the bed. 'Chibcha Indians . . .' he gasped. 'I bet they really know what they're talking about – magic and all that stuff. I bet it's like they said . . . that jumper will improve my brain power. Yes! Great!' Quickly, he pulled the jumper from under the bed and stared at it. 'It looks pretty weird to me and it smells pretty weird, too – but super-natural stuff's got to be different.'

He spread the jumper over his knees and smiled. 'The least I can do is to give it a chance to prove itself. I might come out top of the class – or at least get 40 marks. That'll be good enough for a first try.'

So it was decided. He would wear the jumper tomorrow and keep his fingers crossed that its supernatural powers would work okay. Eric closed his books and stuffed them into his school bag. No point in studying now. Then he lay back on the bed and reached for a copy of *The Match*.

Chapter 4

'Where d'you get it from, Ez?' Wesley asked the next morning.

'South America,' Eric replied casually, pulling the Striped Horror down over his bottom.

'You've never been to South America,' Brent Dwyer interrupted. 'You're always telling lies, you are.'

'Did I say I'd been there?'

'Good as.'

'Well, Creep, it was my auntie who sent it to me. She works there. Right?'

'Anyway, it stinks,' said Brent, gripping his nose between his fingers. 'It smells of donkey droppings.'

A fierce argument raged until the classroom door opened and The Bodge walked in with a pile of test papers in his hands.

'No, talking,' said The Bodge, standing in the doorway. 'Just get out your pens.' Then, as they filed past him, he frowned and twitched his nose the way rabbits do. 'Someone,' he said, staring at their feet. 'Someone has stepped into some dog dirt. Please check the bottoms of your shoes.'

A general titter ran round the room and they all turned up their feet to look.

'Please, Sir,' Brent Dwyer called out. 'It's not dog dirt – it's Eric Braithwaite. He's got a niffy jumper on. It's horrible, Sir.'

The Bodge looked suspiciously across at Eric. He stood up and walked towards him and, as he grew closer, he knew that what Brent Dwyer had said was true.

'Have you been rolling in cow muck, Eric?'

'No, Sir.'

'Then why are you so disgustingly smelly?'

'It's my South American jumper, Sir.'

'South American?'

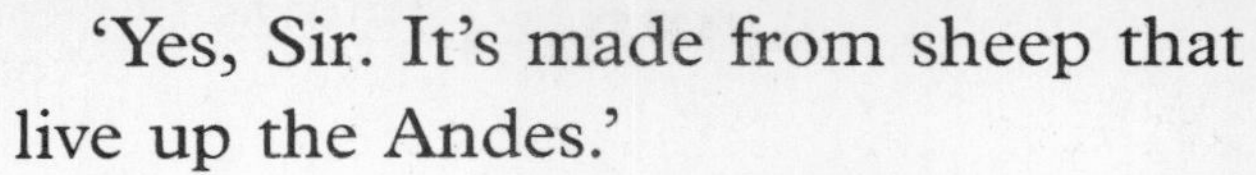

'Yes, Sir. It's made from sheep that live up the Andes.'

'Not made from the SHEEP, Eric. Made from their WOOL possibly,' The Bodge replied. 'But it SMELLS and I think you'd better take it off and put it in the cloakroom before the entire class passes out.'

Eric had not expected this. Now the experiment with the supernatural power would be over before it had begun.

Chapter 5

'Can't take it off, Sir,' said Eric. 'My mum says I've got to keep it on because I've got a weak chest and I'll have to have a month off school if I get an infection like I did last winter.'

'It's not winter,' The Bodge replied in an exasperated tone, 'and you are not likely to get an infection.'

Eric shrugged his shoulders and looked down at his desk.

'Got to do what my mum says,' he insisted. 'You told us we should always do what our mums say, didn't you, Sir?'

The Bodge had no reply to that.

When the bell rang for break, the test was over and their teacher stood at the front of the class and told them the results would be out the following day. Then they would know who would have to go to The Big Cheese for extra lessons.

The next morning, Eric decided to wear the Striped Horror again. In spite of the pong, he liked wearing it and he enjoyed being the centre of attention. 'Where d'you get it from, Ez?' 'Cor! Who d'you know in South America?' 'Is it really made of mountain goats?' Sometimes he had to put them right on a thing or two,

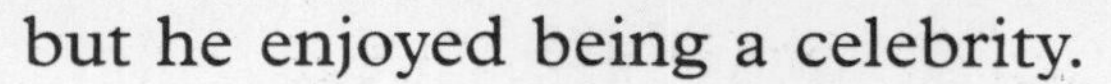

but he enjoyed being a celebrity.

'You know, Ez,' said Wesley as they walked across the playground. 'Your jumper doesn't smell the same today. It's kind of (sniff, sniff) . . . different.'

Eric smiled. 'I sprayed it,' he said.

'What with?'

'I found this can of fly killer under the sink,' he explained. 'Good, isn't it?'

Nobody else thought it was good. Annie Barnstable said she felt sick when she went near him and she had to rush to the lavatory.

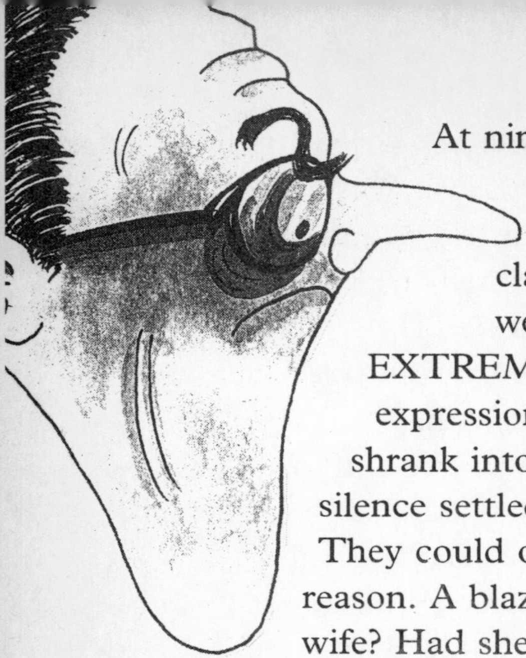

At nine o'clock, when The Bodge walked in the classroom, he was wearing his 'I AM EXTREMELY ANGRY' expression and they all shrank into their seats and silence settled on the class. They could only guess at the reason. A blazing row with his wife? Had she biffed him over the head with a frying pan? Had she made him sleep in the garage? The possibilities were endless.

'I am going to give you back the tests you did yesterday,' he said in clipped tones. Then he began to march up and down the room, flinging the papers on the desks so that they bounced and skidded on the surface.

'Right!' The Bodge commanded when he had finished. 'You may look at your results.'

With crossed fingers, Eric turned his paper over and looked at the first page. Jumping jellyfish! – it was covered in red ticks. And the second page . . . and the third. Not a cross in sight. It was amazing! How could it have happened?

The Striped Horror! It had worked! – just like Auntie Rose said! His brain power had improved no end! Eric sank back in his chair and smiled. He wouldn't have to go for extra lessons. He'd be able to play in the match, after all.

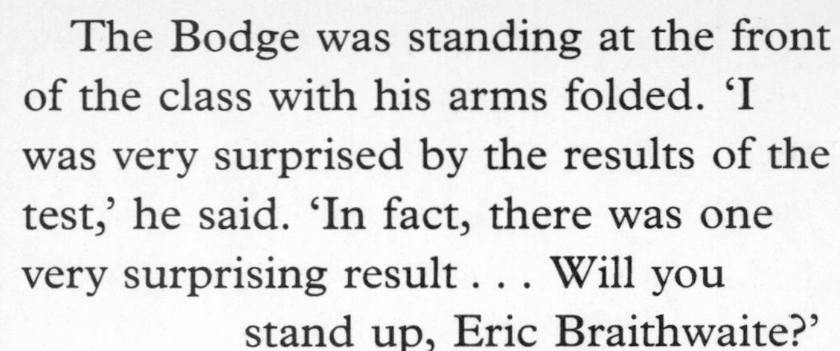

The Bodge was standing at the front of the class with his arms folded. 'I was very surprised by the results of the test,' he said. 'In fact, there was one very surprising result . . . Will you stand up, Eric Braithwaite?'

Eric pulled himself up to his full height and felt his chest fill with pride as twenty-four pairs of eyes fixed on him.

He had never been anywhere near the top of the class before. He smiled at the rows of open mouths and he nodded his head like royalty on the telly. He had full marks and he was thrilled to bursting!

'Something of a surprise, Eric, to see that you have gained one hundred marks.'

The class gasped and began to clap but The Bodge held up his hand for silence.

'In all my years as a teacher,' he continued, 'I have never known anyone gain full marks in one of my tests. And I can only think of one way you could have done it, Eric Braithwaite . . . and that is by CHEATING!'

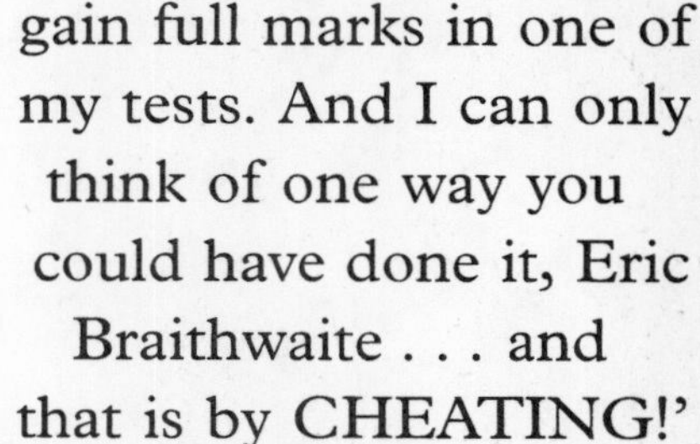

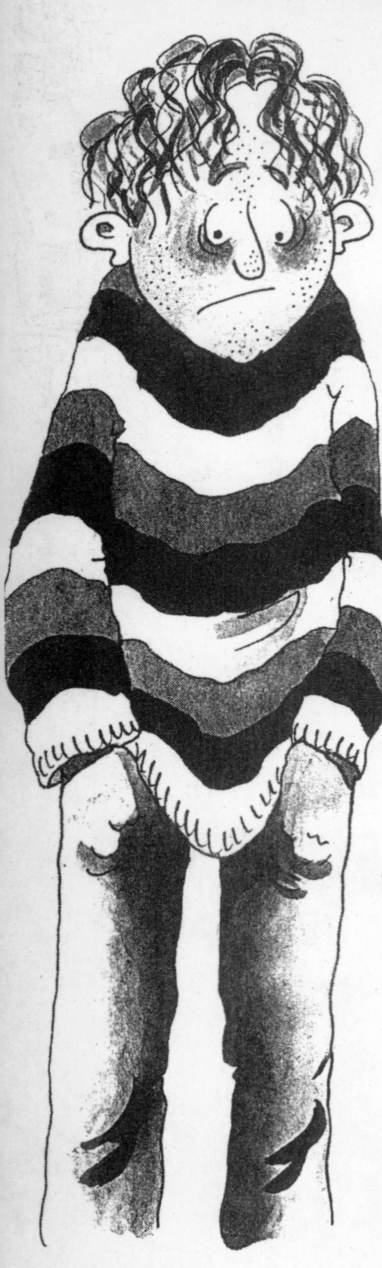

Eric was shocked. He may have cheated in the past but yesterday . . .

'No, Sir! I never!' he protested.

'I can't believe that.'

'I never, honest!'

'Then we shall let Mrs Cracker decide. She is waiting for you in her office. Go at once,' he ordered and Eric, feeling deeply offended, stuffed his hands in his pockets and headed towards the door.

Who was going to believe he had done the test all by himself?

Chapter 6

In the living room of number 34 Corporation Street, Mum sat in an armchair in front of the telly and Eric sat crosslegged on the floor, plates of sausages, chips and mushy peas on their knees.

'I had to go and see the Head this afternoon, Mum,' Eric said as he dipped a sausage into a mound of tomato sauce.

His mum sat up abruptly and rested her fork on her plate. 'You've not been up to your tricks again . . . not after last time.' Then she waved her fork across at her son. 'I've told you before, I won't . . .'

Eric was enjoying himself. For the first time ever, he hadn't been up to anything (except wearing a new jumper). He smiled and slowly chewed on a piece of sausage.

'It was because I came top in the tests,' he said when he had swallowed. 'The Big Cheese says I'm BRILLIANT.'

'Don't talk daft, Eric. And don't call Mrs Cracker "The Big Cheese". It's cheeky.'

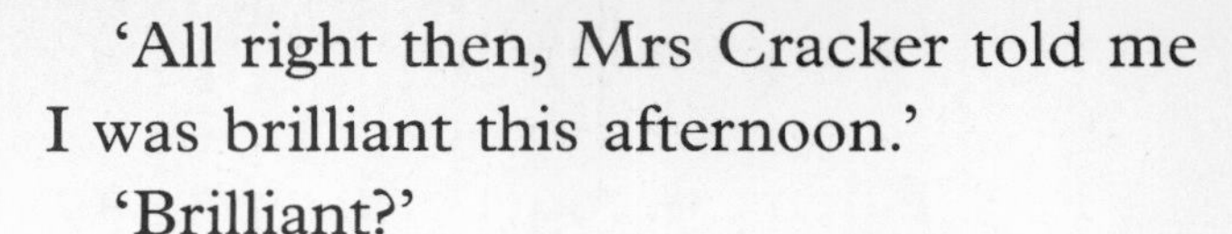

'All right then, Mrs Cracker told me I was brilliant this afternoon.'

'Brilliant?'

'A genius, she reckoned.'

Mum looked doubtful.

'She gave me loads of tests and I got them all right.'

'Never! You're having me on, Eric. You're telling porkies.'

'I'm not, Mum, honest,' Eric protested.

'People don't become brilliant all of a sudden. Pull the other one.'

'Well,' said Eric craftily, 'if you remember, I studied ever so hard the other night, didn't I? No telly – nothing. I just stayed in my room all night and worked.'

'Still doesn't make sense,' she snorted and tried to eat the rest of her tea but somehow she had lost her appetite.

Mrs Braithwaite didn't know what to make of Eric's story. All that night she tossed and turned in bed and, the next morning, she decided to go to

school and sort it out. She wouldn't rest until she had seen Mrs Cracker and heard the truth of the matter.

On the dot of nine o'clock, Mum was sitting white-faced in the head teacher's office with Eric standing next to her. The air was heavy with 'Essence of Old Socks' as The Big Cheese stood behind her mahogany desk, clasping her fingers across her ample bosom.

'What's all this about our Eric being brilliant?' asked Mrs Braithwaite. 'I don't understand it, Mrs Cracker? What's going on?'

The Big Cheese pursed her scarlet lips then leaned back flashing a dazzling smile.

'What's going on is simply a MIRACLE!' she gushed. 'I can hardly believe it myself. You see, Eric has always been outstanding at games but he has never been very good at – er – class work, has he?'

'No. Not exactly VERY good,' Mum said.

'And then, quite out of the blue, he has turned into a GENIUS!'

Eric blushed and looked down at his feet while Mrs Braithwaite's mouth fell open with shock.

'But don't take my word for it, Mrs Braithwaite,' The Big Cheese continued. 'I have the results of tests to prove it.' And she pushed a pile of papers towards her. 'I gave him four extremely difficult tests – here in this room – and he passed them all BRILLIANTLY! He is, without doubt, the most gifted child I have had in my school. EVER!'

Mrs Braithwaite's throat was suddenly dry as a piece of last week's stale bread and she gasped for air. The discovery of her son's brains came as a bombshell!

'But WHY is he brilliant?' she asked when she had recovered herself. 'He's never been brilliant before . . . and it's not as if he comes from a brilliant family. Why is he brilliant all of a sudden? It's not natural!'

The Big Cheese paced backwards and forwards across the pale blue carpet. 'Never mind WHY he has suddenly sprouted brains, Mrs Braithwaite. The fact is, he has – and we should be delighted about it, shouldn't we?'

Eric nodded enthusiastically while Mum leaned back in the chair, quite overcome.

The Big Cheese rested her pear-shaped bottom on the

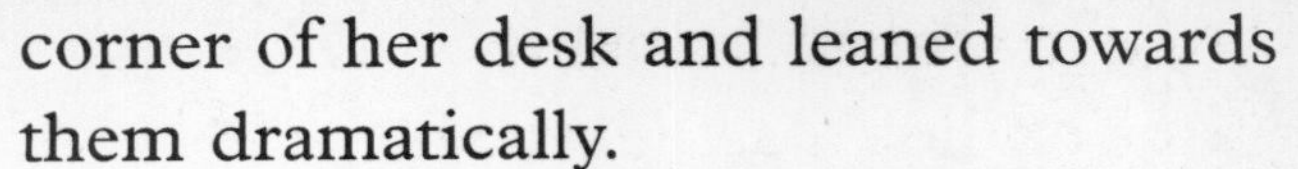

corner of her desk and leaned towards them dramatically.

'Now I have more thrilling news for you both!' she squealed, unable to contain her excitement. 'Last night, I contacted a – er – friend at the BBC.' (At this point she blushed a little.) 'He has agreed that Eric can represent the school in the "Junior Brain of the Year" on television.'

A grin spread across Eric's face like butter on hot toast. But Mrs Braithwaite almost fell off the chair. Her son on the telly? Could it be possible?

'When?' she gasped.

'Next week, actually,' The Big Cheese replied. 'Do your best, Eric, and you may well win a new minibus for the school!' Then she giggled. 'I'm quite excited by it all, aren't you?'

'Great!' Eric replied. 'I might be famous!'

Mrs Braithwaite was more stunned than excited but that evening, when she had got over the shock, she suddenly felt very proud of Eric.

'A son of mine at the BBC!' she said, putting her arm round Eric's shoulder. 'I never thought I'd see the day!'

'I know, Mum,' Eric said bouncing up and down like a bed spring. 'It's great, isn't it? I've always wanted to be on the telly.'

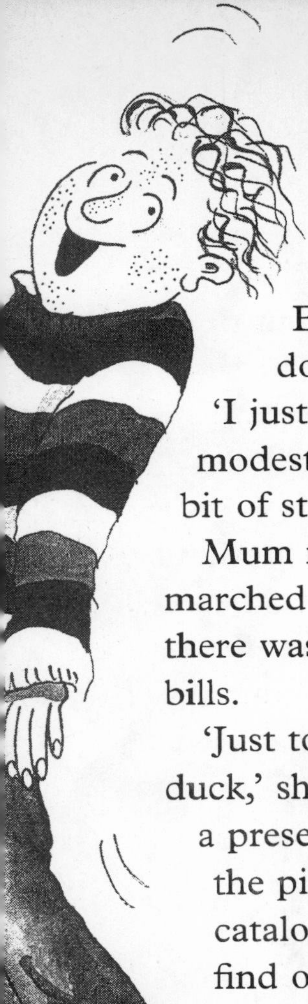

Mum shook her head. 'But how did you get so clever, my duck?'

Eric looked up at her and then down at the Striped Horror. 'I just did my best, Mum,' he said modestly. 'It just goes to show what a bit of studying can do, doesn't it?'

Mum nodded and then suddenly marched over to the sideboard where there was a pile of magazines and old bills.

'Just to show you how pleased I am, duck,' she said, 'I'm going to buy you a present.' She pulled from under the pile a large, mail order catalogue. 'Now let's see if I can find one . . .' And she began to flick through the pages.

Eric jumped on the settee to peer over her shoulder. 'What, Mum, what? Is it that United strip, eh?'

'No it isn't!' she said and pointed to page 256. 'I'm going to buy you a SUIT to wear on the telly. You'll look a treat!'

Eric's face paled to the colour of uncooked dough.

'But I want to wear Auntie Rose's jumper,' he protested. 'It's my lucky jumper.'

Mrs Braithwaite shook her head. 'No way, Eric. Jumpers won't do at the BBC. You don't want to let the school down, do you? A nice smart navy suit and a white shirt – that's what you're having. Just the job.'

Chapter 7

The following week, Eric whizzed off to London with his mum, looking like royalty in his navy suit. He was going to the Television Centre to record the programme in two sessions – the first session in the morning and, if he won through, the final in the afternoon.

When Eric arrived, he found that there were three other contestants in his section – Lavender Trout, Trevor Braine and Michelle Duff. They were all older and looked very brainy and Eric felt as nervous as a cat in a dog kennel.

They had been in reception for ten minutes or so when a woman with a short skirt and big feet came along to collect them. 'Follow me, you guys!' she called out. 'I'll take you to the set. Come on, now. Don't lag behind.'

She marched them down a maze of dimly lit corridors and took them to a white-painted studio about three times the size of a school hall.

Cameras were being pushed into position by blue-jeaned people in headsets and everyone looked busy. Dozens and dozens of red plush seats stretched to the back of the studio and already the audience were walking in and buzzing with excitement.

It was all very well being on the telly, Eric thought, but what if he made a fool of himself? The others were probably brainier than he was. He began to panic and his skin broke out in goose bumps.

His stomach began to churn.

SQUELCH . . . GLURP . . . And suddenly, he felt sick. All those people watching him and – worst of all – the whole school hoping he would win the minibus.

To calm himself, he pushed his fingers in the gap between two of his shirt buttons and felt the Striped Horror underneath.

Straight away, he felt better. (Luckily, the suit and shirt from the catalogue had been too big. 'I'll grow into it, Mum,' he had insisted – and so, on the morning of the competition, he had put the Striped Horror under the shirt . . . and no one had noticed.)

The four competitors stood at the side and watched the finishing touches being put to the set. Then, from the middle of the floor, the voice of the floor manager called, 'All clear now . . . Will you come onto the set, please?'

They all walked towards the purple shell-suited figure who smiled weakly while flapping his hands in the direction of four empty chairs.

'Sit over here, would you, luvvies?' he gushed.

Eric sat in between Trevor Braine and Michelle Duff. Trevor was small and ratty looking and refused to speak to anyone. Michelle on the other hand, was very friendly but she clung to a large

white handkerchief as if her life depended on it and sniffed non-stop.

'My nabe's Bichelle,' she whispered to Eric. 'I'b ever so derbous, are you?'

He wasn't too sure what she had said but he blinked his eyes and nodded anyway.

They had been in their seats for no more than a few minutes when Trevor Braine turned his head and began to glare at Eric. The pong of the Striped Horror had drifted up from under his shirt and reached Trevor's ultra-sensitive nose. The smell would have been no problem to anyone used to the whiff of South American goat dung – but to Trevor Braine it was unbearable. Gradually, his face turned white, then purple and green until he suddenly clapped his hand over his mouth, groaned and rushed off the set.

A voice called down from the control box, 'Somebody go and look after Trevor, will you? We'll have to carry on without him. Okay.'

The purple shell-suit walked over to them. 'Poor old thing,' he said, 'it must have been something he ate. Are you all feeling tickitee boo, luvvies?' They all nodded nervously. 'Then we're ready to roll. KEEP SMILING!'

So that left Lavender, Michelle and Eric.

The background lights dimmed. Bright spotlights focused on the contestants and the opening music played. A door in the back of the set slid open and the presenter, Angela Redruth, walked in to the cheers and applause of the studio audience.

'Tonight, Ladies and Gentlemen, we have the first round in our "Junior Brain of the Year Competition",' she announced as she turned her blue-shadowed eyes on the audience. 'This week, at very short notice, we have included an outstanding young man who could well prove to be one of the country's finest brains. May I introduce you to ten-year-old Eric Braithwaite.'

The audience applauded. Camera 2 zoomed in on Eric's grinning face.

And then the first round began . . .

It soon became clear that Michelle Duff was brighter than all of them. In spite of her sniffles, she was able to answer questions faster than anyone else and, by the end of the first round, she had scored 21.

Lavender, who was very tall and thin, suffered with nerves and her memory had a habit of going blank when she was asked a question. Even so, she managed to gain 12.

Lastly, there was Eric. His nerves affected his voice, making it crack up like a bad telephone line. This slowed him down quite a bit and he only managed to score 9.

'And now for the last round,' Angela Redruth announced. 'Eric, we'll start with you.'

Strangely, he had settled down and was soon answering questions at a belting pace. Five minutes to go and he was neck and neck with Michelle Duff.

Michelle 27 . . . Eric 25
Michelle 29 . . . Eric 28
Michelle 32 . . . Eric 31

. . . until, suddenly, Michelle's sniffles broke out worse than before and turned to sneezes.

Aitchooo! Aitchooo!

Precious seconds were wasted and she dropped a point. Now Eric had an excellent chance of winning.

Everything was going brilliantly – except for one thing. The studio lights. They were beating down like a tropical sun and what with the Striped Horror under his shirt and the heat of his suit, Eric felt like a large bun baking slowly in a hot oven. Sweat trickled down the side of his face and his neck was locked in the grip of his collar. His eyes suddenly felt heavy and he leaned forward on the desk finding

it difficult to stay awake.

Angela Redruth turned to him. 'Eric Braithwaite, your last question . . .'

Eric's head was spinning with the heat and his vision was beginning to blur.

Then Angela said, 'What proportion of the earth's surface is covered in water?'

Eric dug his nails into the palms of his hands as the question swam around in his brain, searching for the answer.

'I think . . .' he hesitated. 'I think the answer is 71%.'

The audience was silent waiting for Angela to speak.

'Correct!' she said.

At once, wild cheers and riotous applause broke out. Eric was the winner. But he didn't hear a thing.

He was so overcome with the heat and the excitement, he had fainted clean away.

Chapter 8

Eric woke up in a small, white room that smelled of disinfectant. He was lying on a couch in his underpants and his Superman vest.

'Is it any wonder you passed out, duck?' his mother said as he opened his eyes. 'You were dressed for the Arctic Circle! Why did you wear that smelly old jumper? You were nearly boiled alive.'

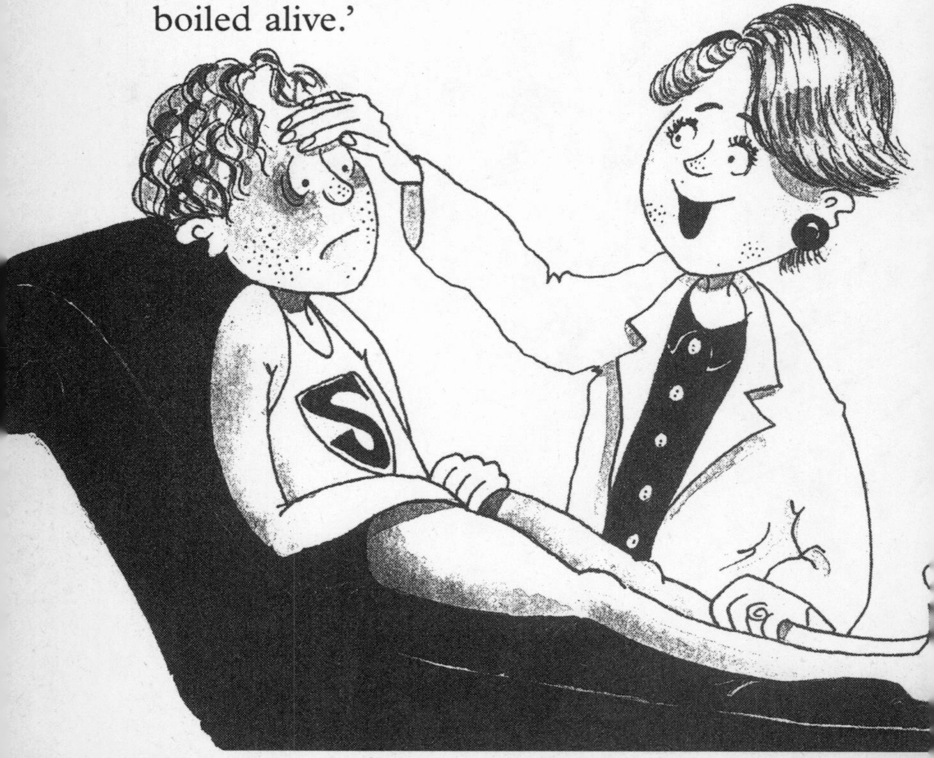

The door opened and Angela Redruth breezed in. 'Feeling better, Eric?' She leaned across the couch and smiled a wide, scarlet smile. 'It's all been a bit much for you, hasn't it?'

Eric nodded weakly.

'Do you want to skip the final this afternoon?' she asked. 'The producer will quite understand if you feel like going back home. It might be best. Michelle can always take your place.'

Eric sat up on the couch. Give in? No way! He wanted to win that minibus for the school. Anyway, he'd look a real wimp if he went home now.

'Don't worry,' he said. 'I'll be okay.'

'Good,' Angela replied. 'Then you've got just over two hours. I suggest you have a good sleep.'

When she had gone, Eric lay thankfully back on the pillow and closed his eyes. For the next two hours, he slept and dreamed of playing for United.

When he woke up, it was time to get dressed and Mum handed him his suit and then his shirt – neat and newly folded.

'They made a good job of the shirt, didn't they?' she said. 'Angela insisted on taking it down to the wardrobe department for washing.'

'It didn't need washing,' Eric protested. 'It was clean on this morning.'

'Ah!' said Mum mysteriously. 'That was before the accident.'

'What accident?'

She looked embarrassed. 'It was all a bit of a rush when you fainted, you see. I dumped some of your clothes on that old radiator.'

'And?'

'They fell down the back and got stuck. I managed to fish them out – but they were filthy. I don't suppose they ever clean behind them. Terrible! They were black!'

‘They?’

‘Your shirt and your jumper.’

Suddenly, Eric was filled with alarm.

‘My jumper,’ he said. ‘Where is it?’

His mother smiled as she helped him into his shirt. ‘It’s all right, duck. The lady from wardrobe said it would be dry by the time we go home. So don’t you worry – you’ve not lost it. I know it’s your favourite.’

Eric clamped his hand over his eyes and leaned against the wall for support. It was his worst nightmare. Without the Striped Horror, he'd probably make a fool of himself in front of thousands of viewers.

The only thing to do was to make a run for it.

Suddenly, the door opened. 'Time to record the final, Eric,' said the purple shell-suit. 'If you'll come with me, I'll take you back to the studio.'

Chapter 9

The background lights dimmed. Bright spotlights focused on the four finalists and the opening music played. Angela Redruth walked onto the set like before and did her usual introduction.

And then the last round of the Junior Brain of the Year began.

The other three finalists went before Eric. The questions were even harder than those in the first round of the competition but everyone answered correctly. Full marks.

Then came Eric.

'Your first question,' Angela said in a clear, crisp tone. 'Can you name the planets in the Solar System?'

Eric looked at Angela with a confident smile and opened his mouth to answer.

'Ergggghhhh . . .'

A peculiar noise came out of his throat. He tried again.

'Urrrrgggg . . .'

No words came. Just a grunt. And Eric blushed with embarrassment.

'Do have a drink of water, Eric, and we'll start again,' Angela said sympathetically.

Eric reached for the glass and gulped it down.

'TAKE TWO,' called out the floor manager.

'ROLLING!'

Angela smiled as if nothing had happened. 'And now for your first question, Eric. Who were the daughters of Henry the Eighth?'

'Arrrhhhggg . . .'

'CUT!' the floor manager yelled and flapped his arms madly as a signal to the cameraman.

Suddenly, Eric was surrounded by people wanting to know what was wrong. He grabbed a pencil and wrote I CAN'T SAY A WORD. MY VOICE WON'T WORK.

'Nerves,' said Angela Redruth, turning to a man with a red beard who was looking furious.

'I knew he should have gone home after he fainted this morning,' he said. 'We'll just have to get Michelle Duff to take his place.'

Everyone was very sympathetic and Eric was led off the set and settled in a chair until a car arrived to take him home.

'I'll see he's looked after,' Mum said as they waved goodbye. 'I expect it's the excitement. He's not used to all this fuss, you see.'

And Eric sighed a deep sigh of relief. He had escaped.

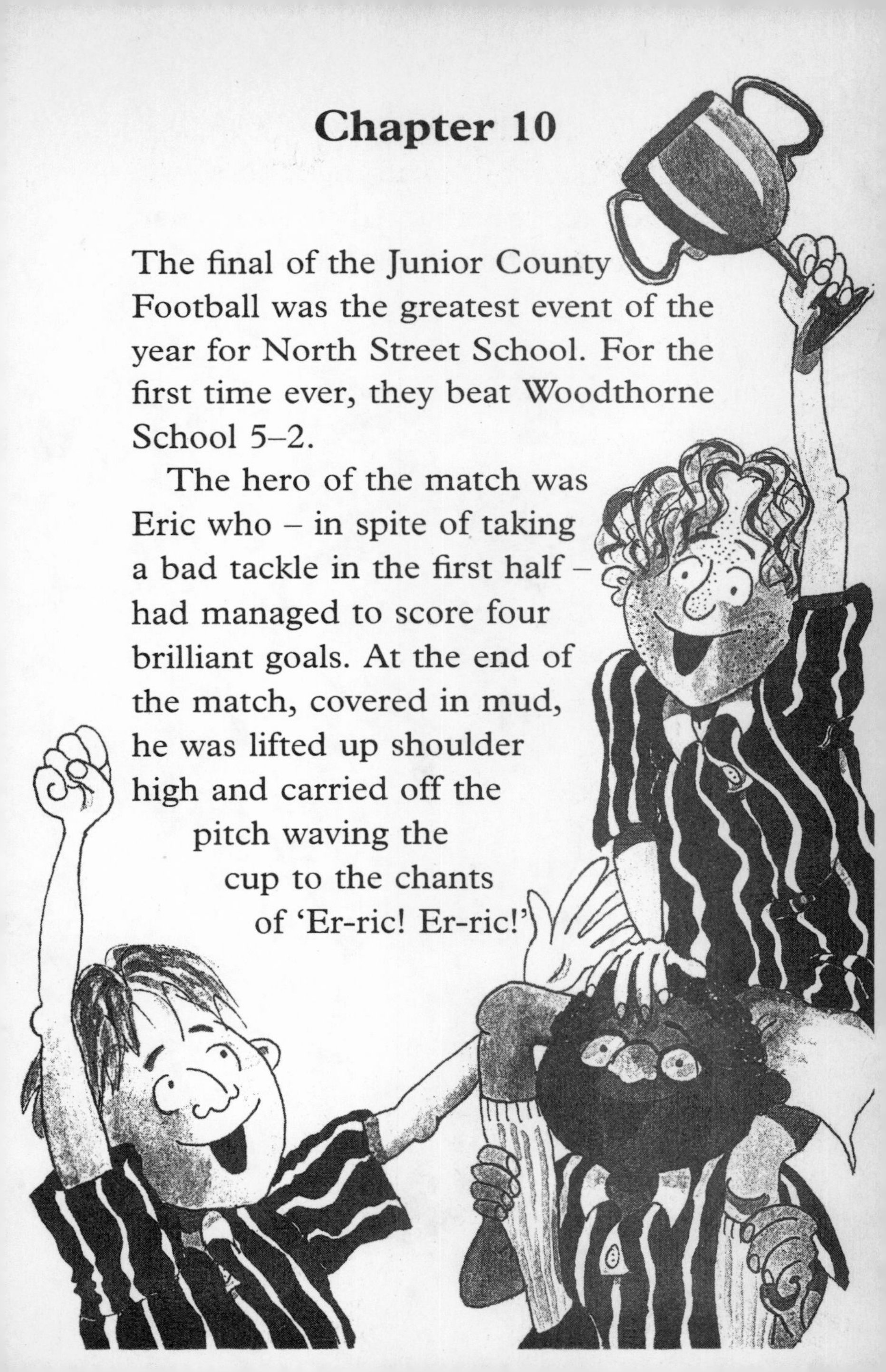

Chapter 10

The final of the Junior County Football was the greatest event of the year for North Street School. For the first time ever, they beat Woodthorne School 5–2.

The hero of the match was Eric who – in spite of taking a bad tackle in the first half – had managed to score four brilliant goals. At the end of the match, covered in mud, he was lifted up shoulder high and carried off the pitch waving the cup to the chants of 'Er-ric! Er-ric!'

Even The Bodge was pleased with the team and The Big Cheese was ecstatic! She barged into the changing room without

so much as a 'May I come in?' and shouted, 'Well, done, everyone! Super! Terrific! Mr Hodgetts and I are so proud of you all,' she said, clasping her hands dramatically. 'Particularly our captain, Eric Braithwaite, after his disappointment in the television competition. You are a true champion, Eric.'

When all the excitement died down, Eric walked home with Wesley. 'I'll tell you what, Wez,' he said. 'I'd rather have a football competition any day.'

'Better than Brain of the Year?'

'Loads better.'

'Better than the telly?'

'Well, all that being famous isn't all it's cracked up to be.'

'How d'you mean?'

'I mean, it's good to be normal and walk down the street without being stared at or asked for my autograph. Know what I mean?'

'I think so, Ez.'

'It's all very well being in the papers –

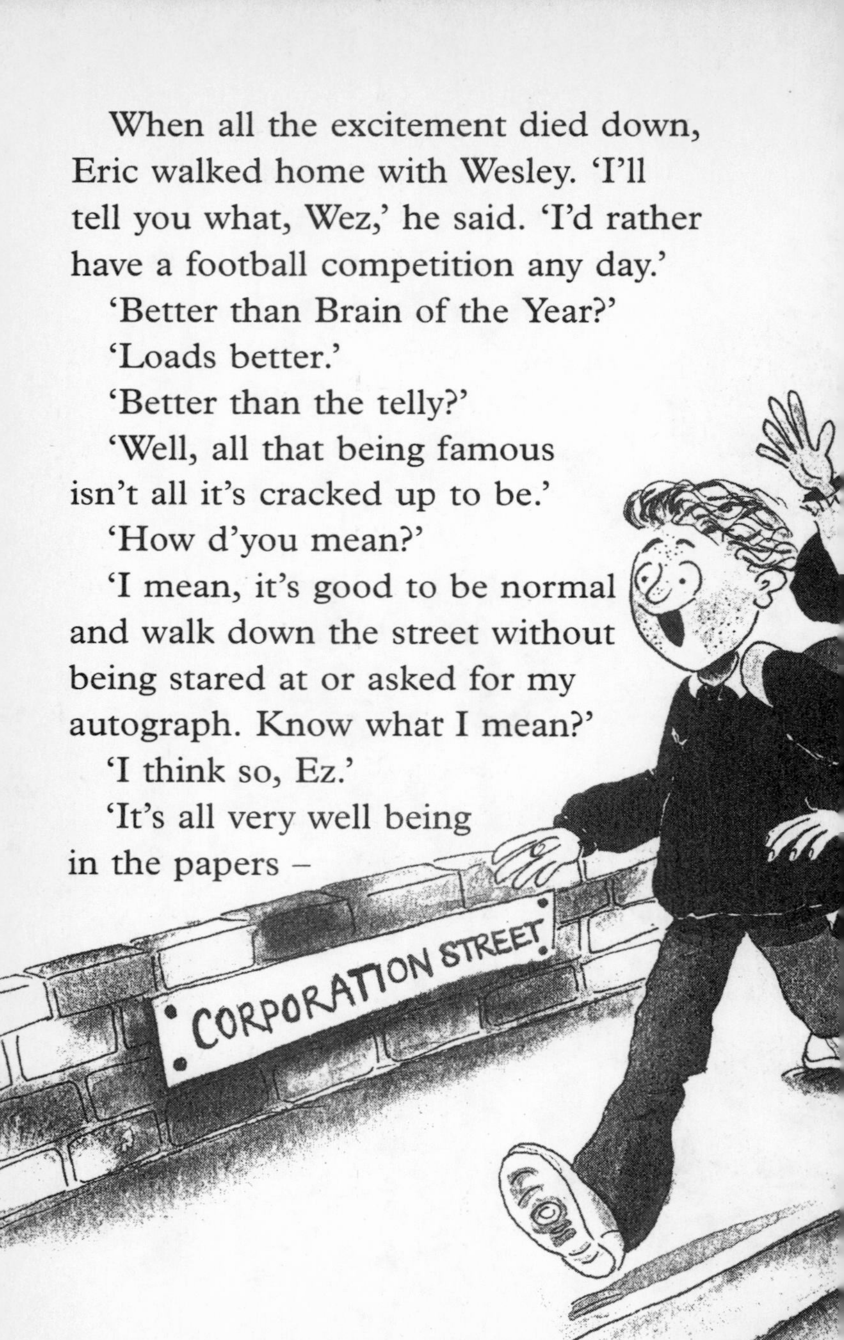

but I'd rather be . . . ordinary.'

'You . . . ordinary? Never!'

'Well.'

'You're great at football.'

'Do you reckon?'

''Course I do!' said Wez and slapped Eric on the back.

When they came to the top of Corporation Street, they parted company. 'See you, Wez!' Eric called and ran down the hill towards home.

Mum was in the kitchen frying bacon.

'We won!' Eric yelled as he burst through the door. '5 – 2 and guess who got four of 'em?'

'Brilliant!' she said and gave him a hug. 'Now isn't that better than all the telly competitions in the world? Who needs 'em?'

'Yeah! Who needs 'em!'

'By the way, duck,' she said as she cracked an egg into the pan, 'there's a parcel for you.'

Eric found it on the hall table, wrapped in brown paper and addressed in Aunt Rose's unmistakable bold black writing. Five stamps were stuck in the corner, post-marked *Cali – Rep. of Colombia . . .*